The people of Etheria love their Princess Adora, who is gentle and good. But there are times when the country is in danger and they need someone of strength to lead them. Those are the times when Princess Adora takes sword in hand to become She-Ra, Princess of Power. She rides Swift Wind, her magical winged unicorn, and defends her country and her people against the forces of evil.

British Library Cataloguing in Publication Data

Grant, John,
    Shadow weaver's magic mirror. — (She-Ra Princess of Power. Series 857; v. 2)
    I. Title   II. Davies, Robin, *1950-*   III. Series
    823'.914[J]   PZ7
    ISBN 0-7214-0958-X

First edition

Published by Ladybird Books Ltd Loughborough Leicestershire UK
Ladybird Books Inc Lewiston Maine 04240 USA

SHE-RA
PRINCESS of POWER

Shadow Weaver's
Magic Mirror

by John Grant
illustrated by Robin Davies

Ladybird Books

Hordak sat in his stronghold plotting yet again to defeat the rebels of Etheria. He had a huge and powerful army, but time and again they had been beaten by the rebels under their leader, She-Ra.

In a swirl of darkness Shadow Weaver, Mistress of Dark Magic appeared in the room.

"You are wasting your time," she said. "You think that because your warriors are trained to fight, and have good weapons, that is all they need to beat the Light Folk. But I know better. Every enemy has a weakness. Theirs is the very light which is the secret of their strength. With some magic of my own, I will use the light to help you beat them once and for all."

5

In a secret underground chamber, Shadow Weaver had constructed a magic mirror. She showed it to Hordak.

"A mirror!" he cried. "Is that *all*?"

"This is not just *any* mirror!" cried Shadow Weaver. "The people of the shadows have worked for a year and a day to polish it to perfection. It is made from rare lumenite crystal. It needs only my magic to turn it into a weapon of great power. But first, it must be placed in position."

"A mirror for a weapon," grumbled Hordak. "A battery of stun-cannon would be better."

All the same, he ordered a gang of his warriors to carry the mirror up to the surface. At Shadow Weaver's command, they carried it to Whispering Wood and set it up beside a forest track that passed through a clearing.

Then Hordak and Shadow Weaver hid themselves in a patch of briar nearby.

While Hordak and Shadow Weaver were busy with the magic mirror, Madame Razz was also busy with magic in another part of the wood. She was trying to improve some of the wild flowers...by making them bigger. So far it hadn't worked.

The Twiggets watched from a tree. Kowl watched from a tree a little farther away. He didn't trust

Madame Razz's magic. It too often went wrong. She had already made it snow, caused one of the Twiggets to float upwards like a balloon, and turned Broom into a toadstool.

Kowl moved even farther back. "Most people get *better* with practice," he thought — but not Madame Razz.

Madame Razz waved her arms, twirled round three times, and began again.

9

Then she pointed to a buttercup in the grass and cried,

"SUN AND WIND, SAND AND SEA!
IN THE FOREST...GREATEST BE!"

For a moment nothing happened, then with a loud and angry buzz a bumblebee the size of a Twigget rose into the air.

"Oh, dear!" cried Madame Razz, "I meant 'BE', not 'BEE'!"

She said a magic word and the bee became small again and went on its way muttering, "Nobody will believe a word of this back at the hive!"

Kowl decided to go before Madame Razz did anything more dreadful. He spread his wings and flew away through the wood.

Kowl swooped between the trees and across a clearing. There was a track, and to one side he saw something very odd.

"If I didn't know better," he said to himself, "I'd say that there was a large picture frame over there. But I *do* know better. Picture frames don't grow on trees. And people don't usually leave them lying around in Whispering Wood."

He stood and thought for a moment. "I ought to take a closer look, but Madame Razz's magic has made me a bit nervous. I'll find someone to take a look with me."

Keeping well clear of the strange object, Kowl flew on. He met Glimmer out walking, and told her what he had seen.

"You are a bit of an old silly," she said, smiling, "but if you want, I will come with you and we can look at this strange thing together."

Kowl still felt nervous. He hoped that the mysterious picture frame might have vanished, or that the owner might have come and taken it away. But it was still there, half-hidden by the trees.

Kowl stayed on the track while Glimmer went on. She stopped and called back, "It's not a picture frame, it's a mirror. Someone has set up a big mirror. What a strange thing to do. I wonder why?"

In the cover of the briar patch Shadow Weaver hissed to Hordak, "Any moment now she'll find out!"

Glimmer stood in front of the mirror. She looked at her reflection, and smiled. Her reflection smiled back at her. Then – it did something else. It stepped out of the mirror and stood looking at her.

"A clever trick," whispered Hordak.

"It is only just beginning," replied Shadow Weaver. "Watch!"

Astounded, Glimmer asked, "Who are you?"

"Why, I'm Glimmer," replied the reflection.

"You can't be!" cried Glimmer. "My mother, Queen Angella, only has one daughter...me!"

The reflection laughed, and it was Glimmer's laugh that Kowl heard.

14

But there was worse to come.

Glimmer and her reflection stood side by side so that they were both reflected in the mirror. Both reflections now stepped out. There were now FOUR Glimmers!

Glimmer called, "Help me, Kowl!" The others did the same! Kowl could no longer tell which was the real Glimmer, especially as more and more stepped from the mirror.

"I'll get help!" called Kowl.

"Please hurry!" cried all the Glimmers together.

As Kowl flew as fast as he could to get help, Hordak and Shadow Weaver shrieked with glee.

"A few more in the trap," laughed Hordak, "and they will be so busy working out who is who that they will have no time to meddle in my affairs!"

*　　*　　*

Kowl found Princess Adora watering her horse at a stream. Quickly he told her what had happened.

"This is the work of Shadow Weaver, without a doubt," said Adora.

Kowl gladly perched behind the princess on Spirit, and showed her the way to the magic mirror. When they were almost there, they dismounted and crept through the trees. Things were even worse than Kowl had left them.

The mirror was almost hidden by a huge crowd of girls, all looking exactly like Princess Glimmer. There were even some birds and small animals which had strayed too close to the magic mirror.

Adora called, "Glimmer, which one is the real you?"

"*I* am," they all called back at once.

20

A wild cry of laughter made Adora look round. From the cover of the briar patch Hordak cried, "Join your friend, Princess! Etheria would be all the better for an army of Princess Adoras! Perhaps I can help you to make up your mind!"

He fired a bolt from his energy weapon. Adora dived for cover behind a tree. "This," she thought, "is a task for She-Ra, Princess of Power!"

Leaving Kowl to keep an eye on things, Adora hurried to where she had left Spirit. Drawing her sword, she cried,

"FOR THE HONOUR OF GRAYSKULL!"

In an instant she was transformed to She-Ra, Princess of Power. In a blaze of mystic light, Spirit became Swift Wind, the winged unicorn.

Leaping to the saddle, She-Ra cried, "UP, SWIFT WIND!"

High above the tree-tops, She-Ra looked down
upon the crowded clearing. There seemed to be
even *more* Glimmers now, but she had a clear view
of the strange mirror. Putting Swift Wind into a steep
dive, she aimed her sword and let loose a stream of
light energy. It hit the target squarely, but the mirror
didn't break! The energy bounced back, and She-Ra
swerved as it just missed her.

She-Ra fired again, and again. But it was no use.

From the ground, Shadow Weaver shrieked up at
her, "Your weapon is useless against my magic!"

She-Ra didn't waste time replying. She had an
idea. The weapons of the Light Folk might be

powerless against Shadow Weaver's magic mirror, but was it proof against a simple weapon...like an arrow, for instance?

She brought Swift Wind to earth close to where Kowl waited. "We must find Bow, the Master Archer," she said. "You go that way! I'll go this!"

Kowl flapped off through the trees, while Swift Wind again rose into the air carrying She-Ra on the search for the Master Archer.

Kowl had not gone far when he found Madame Razz, who was still trying to get her spell right. At the moment she had managed to get flowers sprouting all over Broom. He didn't seem very pleased.

Kowl landed on the ground beside Broom and Madame Razz. He nodded to Broom. "Very pretty," he said politely. "Have you by any chance seen Bow? It's rather urgent. An emergency, really!"

"Bow? No, I can't say I've seen him. An emergency, you say! Perhaps I can help! Nothing like a spot of magic in times of trouble!" said Madame Razz.

"Thanks," said Kowl, "but I must really get on. I must find Bow."

And he flew off again.

She-Ra found Bow as he was holding archery practice for the men of Etheria.

"Energy weapons have no effect on the mirror," she explained. "But, surely an arrow will smash it to pieces."

"I'll try," he said. He dismissed the archers and sprang up behind She-Ra on Swift Wind's back.

They circled the clearing while Bow drew an arrow and fitted it to the bow string. Swift Wind hovered as Bow took aim.

There came a shout from below. Hordak had seen
Bow. He was about to fire his energy weapon at the
Master Archer, but Shadow Weaver stopped him.
"Let them try," she cried. "What harm can a simple
peasant with a stick and a piece of string do?"

Then, Bow loosed the arrow!

The arrow flew over the heads of the crowd in the clearing and hit the mirror. But – the mirror was unharmed, while the arrow was smashed to splinters. Bow fired another arrow. And again another. The mirror was not even scratched.

Shadow Weaver gave a mocking laugh. "Waste your precious arrows!" she cried. "My magic is proof against the most powerful weapon you can find!"

Bow drew another arrow. "No," said She-Ra. "Shadow Weaver is right. There is nothing we can do against this evil thing. The time has come to seek help. The only hope is the Sorceress, who gave me my super-powers."

At a safe distance from the clearing, she set Swift Wind down. Then drawing her sword, she held it aloft and sent her thoughts through space and time to the Sorceress.

At first nothing happened. Then the sword began to glow. And She-Ra heard in her mind the voice of the Sorceress far off in distant Eternia.

"What do you seek of me, She-Ra, Princess of Power?"

"Shadow Weaver has made a magic mirror. It is an evil thing, but our weapons are useless against it."

She-Ra felt the Sorceress in her mind. Then the voice came again. "I will send you the Arrow of Apollo, fashioned when the Universe was young. Nothing can resist its power. Use it well. There will be no second chance."

Then the voice of the Sorceress faded, and all was silent.

A beam of blinding light appeared in the sky. It shone down through the trees, and was so bright that She-Ra and Bow covered their eyes and Swift Wind backed away in fear.

Then as quickly as it had appeared, the strange light began to fade. It grew dimmer, and at last was gone altogether. On the ground where the light had shone lay an arrow. It seemed almost to be made out of light itself.

Bow picked it up, and could feel how it glowed with power.

"It all depends on you, now," said She-Ra. "We haven't a moment to lose!"

Once again Swift Wind rose into the air carrying
She-Ra and Bow, and the precious Arrow of Apollo.

As Swift Wind swooped once more over the
clearing, Hordak gave a great shout. "Don't those
fools ever learn? That simpleton with the bow still
thinks that he can destroy the mirror!"

But Shadow Weaver had caught a glimpse of the arrow which Bow was drawing back. "Stop him!" she cried. "He has somehow come into possession of magic even more powerful than mine!"

Hordak raised his weapon to fire. But he was too late. The arrow was on its way. In a streak of dazzling light it struck the centre of the mirror. With a flash brighter than a hundred suns, and a sound like a thunderclap, the magic mirror vanished!

Glimmer stood alone among the trees. She looked dazed, but unhurt.

Swift Wind came down in the clearing, and She-Ra ran towards Glimmer.

"I feel as if I've been asleep," said Glimmer. "What happened?"

"You fell into one of Shadow Weaver's evil traps," She-Ra told her. "Thanks to Bow and the Sorceress, you are safe."

"Only for the time being!" came Hordak's voice. "You have been lucky to escape this time. There will come a time when there will be no shining arrows and other tricks to protect you!"

"Remember," cried Shadow Weaver, "no one escapes for ever from the power of my dark magic!"

"Did someone say 'magic'?" It was Madame Razz. "I heard there was an emergency," she said. "But it seems to be over."

She came swooping into the clearing on Broom.
"I've got it right at last," she cried. "See! I'll show
you!"

She twirled round and waved her arms. Then she
cried,

"EARTH AND WATER, WIND AND FIRE!
GROW HIGHER...HIGHER...
HIGHER...HIGHER!"

And nothing happened.

She tried again,
   "OAK, ASH AND THORN!
    ELM, BEECH AND BRIAR!"

And this time it worked, although perhaps not quite how Madame Razz intended! The briar thicket around Hordak and Shadow Weaver began to grow!

The briar branches grew thicker and taller. The thorns grew sharper and longer. Hordak and Shadow Weaver became entangled as they struggled to get free, but it was no use.

Roaring with rage, Hordak blasted his way out in a cloud of smoke and flame, over the tree-tops and away.

Shadow Weaver vanished in a swirl of shadow back to her dark lair.

"Oh, dear!" exclaimed Madame Razz. "I got it wrong again!"

"Not at all, Madame Razz," laughed She-Ra. "This time you got it absolutely right!"